3J

P9-CEA-825

TOP SECRET

Amelia's
Notebook

by
Marissa Moss
(and, of course, ME, Amelia!)

DO NOT OPEN

DANGER: RADIOACTIVE

ALLSTON BRANCH LIBRARY
American Girl™

This notebook is dedicated to
Simon,
who knows how to be a great friend,
and to Journal Writers Everywhere.

That means this is MY book!

This means no peeking, no copying, no copycatting. So there!

Very nice people work here

Pleasant Company
Publications
8400 Fairway Place
Middleton, Wisconsin
53562

Book Design by Amelia

Who is this character, anyway?

Library of Congress Cataloging-in-Publication Data

Moss, Marissa.
Amelia's Notebook / Marissa Moss.
p. cm.
Summary: The hand-lettered contents of a nine-year-old girl's notebook, in which she records her thoughts and feelings about moving, starting school, and dealing with her older sister, as well as keeping her old best friend and making a new one.
ISBN 1-56247-785-4   ISBN 1-56247-784-6 (pbk.)
[1. Moving, Household — Fiction. 2. Sisters — Fiction. 3. Friendship — Fiction.
4. Schools — Fiction. 5. Diaries — Fiction.]
I. Title.
PZ7. M8538 Am 1999
[Fic] — dc21

98-40671
CIP
AC

It says fiction, but it's the TRUTH!

Originally published by Tricycle Press
First Pleasant Company Publications printing, 1999

An Amelia™ Book

I mean, notebook!

Bonjour!?

Manufactured in Singapore

99 00 01 02 03 04 TWP 10 9 8 7 6 5 4 3 2 1

phone cord — This is for you, Elias!

This is not my phone number. Don't call "X"!

These things all have the same shape

↗ worm

↗ toothpaste

↗ hairdo

suitcases, all packed up

My mom just gave me this notebook. She said it would make me feel better to write down my thoughts. Why would a dumb notebook make me feel better? NOTHING can make me feel better. Except going back home, to my old house, not this new house, in a new city, in a new state.

I almost lost my glow-in-the-dark yo yo. It was under the bed.

I HATE IT HERE ! ! ! ! ! !

Moving was ~~weird~~ weird. A big truck came to our house, and everything, EVERYTHING, went inside it. All our furniture and clothes and dishes and vacuum (is that spelled right?) cleaner. Even my collection of rubber bands, all colors,

Why do I always spell this word wrong? Why does weird look so weird?

piles and piles of boxes with all our STUFF in them

Then the house was empty and sad. I said good-bye to my bedroom. Actually, it's Cleo's bedroom, too. I mean, it was Cleo's bedroom, too.

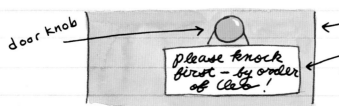

door knob

please knock first - by order of Cleo !

my bedroom door (but not any more)

sign on door knob (this got packed up, too.)

GGnnaagrakk! GGnnaangaagg

our old house →

our old mailbox ↓

SOLD

our old tree ←

Cleo is excited about moving because in the new house she doesn't have to share a bedroom with me anymore. We each get our own. Which is just fine with me! I'm sick of her stuck-up snootiness!

Cleo, with her big lips and jelly roll nose. That's why I call her Jelly Roll Nose. She hates it! →

PFFTTTI

She thinks she's Miss Perfect, just because she happened to be born first. But I know secrets about her that show she's not so perfect. Like she snores, and she picks her nose with her little finger!

← Cleo snoring. Boring!

oooh, yuucch! →

I gave her this watch last year. Is she grateful? No!

Cleo didn't cry when we left. But I did.

← tears

Bare windows, no curtains even. ↓

I picked this wallpaper myself. →

closet door

my old room all EMPTY.

mysterious stain on rug from my volcano science project. →

outlet for plug. My lamp went here.

Then we piled into the car, and it took **3** days to drive to the new house.

This is called perspective, if you draw from an angle. It's tricky!

At every single restaurant we stopped at for lunch or dinner, Cleo ordered the EXACT SAME thing. Hamburger and French fries. EVERY TIME!! Boooooooring!

I told her she was going to turn into a BIG FAT hamburger. She was already beginning to smell like one. She just laughed at me and stuck French fries up her nose till Mom said to quit it.

← Ketchup bottle from below

Ketchup bottle from above. That's easy.

old gum

I saved matches from each restaurant. Now I have a collection.

Cleo making faces at me with French fries up her nose.

m's ☕

(415) 333-212?

MEX

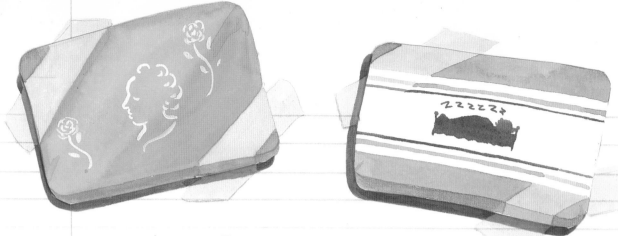

And I saved little soaps from the hotels.

I would have three cute little soaps, but Cleo took one.

The best part about moving (the only good part about moving) was eating in restaurants and staying in hotels. At hotels I don't have to make my bed, I can leave towels on the floor, I can jump up and down on the bed, and, best of all, I can watch CABLE TV!!! Hip Hip Hooray!!

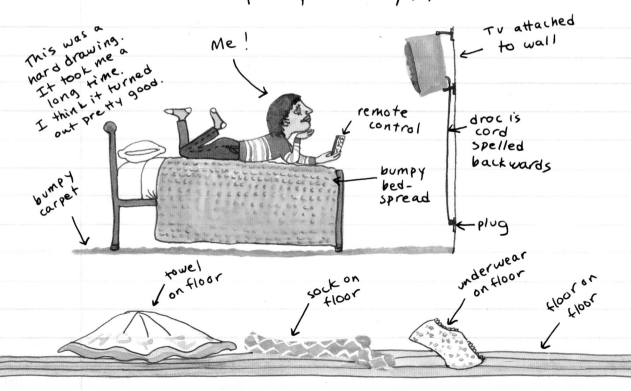

This was a hard drawing. It took me a long time. I think it turned out pretty good.

Me!

TV attached to wall

remote control

droc is cord spelled backwards

bumpy bed-spread

plug

bumpy carpet

towel on floor

sock on floor

underwear on floor

floor on floor

The worst part was everyday I got further and further away from home. I already miss my house, my school, and especially my best friend, Nadia.

My best friend, Nadia
She has braces on her teeth so usually she smiles with her mouth closed. I'm drawing her with her mouth open, because I like her shiny braces. They look like tiny railroad tracks. Or a zipper.

Jello mush

cookie crumbs on the braces train

train tracks

mouth zipper
(Nadia doesn't need one. (Cleo does!)!

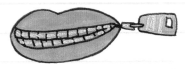

these are teeth

Nadia promised to write lots of letters, and she gave me a great going-away present. It's a set of markers, 24 colors. I'm using them in this notebook and when I write to her. I've already written her 6 postcards.

She gave me some stamps, too, to mail my letters with.

Forget-me-not
U.S. 29¢

Postcard 1 (top, Poobah Lake):

Poobah Lake
A great vacation spot ●

Dear Nadia,
  I'm tired of driving in the car all day and playing travel bingo w/ Cleo. I hope the _l tonight will have swi___ ___h a ___ ing ___ m___

Stamp: Eat Broccoli Week 29¢ Yum!

Nadia Kurz
61 South St.
Barton, CA
  91010

x x o x x o x x o x x o

♡ ♡ ♡

Postcard 2 (Dino-Land):

DINO-LAND
Prehistoric wonders in a scenic park.

Dear Nadia,
  I counted 386 cows today. Booooooring!! But Mom says tomorrow we'll be there. At last!! After all this, it better be worth ___

P.P.

Poodleickus

Nadia Kurz
61 South St.
Barton, CA
  91010

I miss you infinity much.
Do you miss me?
love, x x x o x x
  amelia
♡ ♡

Postcard 3 (bottom):

Dear Nadia,
I still like eating in restaurants, except Cleo drives me crazy. She has hamburgers & French fries every time! She even smells like a hamburger and her skin is turning the color of pasty raw French fries!

Stamp: AMERICAN TRADITIONS HIGH HEELS 29¢

Nadia Kurz
61 South St.
Barton, CA
  91010

♡ I miss you!
u R 2 sweet 2 B 4gotten!
♡ ♡ ♡ love, xxox
  amelia

California map postcard:

Greetings from
CALIFORNIA

• EUREKA   MT. SHASTA
REDWOOD TREES
LASSEN
SUTTER'S FORT
NAPA
GOLD SACRAMENTO
WINE
LAKE TAHOE
the Golden State
STATE FLOWER
GOLDEN GATE BRIDGE
• SAN JOSE
REDWOOD FORESTS
GOLDEN POPPY
FARM LAND
DEATH VALLEY
• PASADENA
MOVIES
• LOS ANGELES
DESERT
S. BARBARA
PAC.

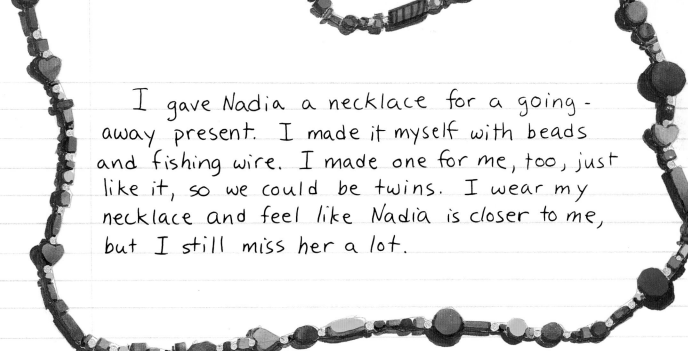

I gave Nadia a necklace for a going-away present. I made it myself with beads and fishing wire. I made one for me, too, just like it, so we could be twins. I wear my necklace and feel like Nadia is closer to me, but I still miss her a lot.

We finally made it to our new house, and after we had lunch at Burger Bob's, the moving truck came with all our stuff. It's an ok house, I guess. Cleo is busy decorating her new room, putting up posters and making a big deal about arranging her furniture.

↑
Cleo's
LAST
hamburger

I just told Mom to put my stuff anywhere, I don't care. I just want to lie in my bed and look out the window. I wish I could turn into a bird and fly back home.

tree branches

me

new window, no curtains yet

DO NOT REMOVE mattress tag or you're under arrest

socket, just like my old room. But that's all that's the same.

house
mean barking dog
follow the dotted line
← school

I wrote Nadia about my new school. It's just two blocks from our house.

Brillo pad hair

Mrs. Kravitz, the music teacher. She has lots of wrinkles. She always says, "Ah-one, Ah-two, Ah-choo!"

glasses chain

SAVE OUR HEDGEHOGS
29¢
U.S.

stamp for Nadia's letter

She always wears a bow.

Ms. Jenko, the PE teacher. She's pretty and chews gum and says, "Come on, gals, let's move those tushes."

and a whistle.

noodles >

Mr. Nudel's noodle

Mr. Nudel, my regular teacher. He smiles a lot and tells funny jokes and waves his arms around. At first I didn't like him, but now I do.

Now, class, I know you can do this. Just do like Mr. Nudel says — don't noodle around and always use your noodle. Nu?

The other kids are alright.
But there's nobody like
Nadia here.

Leah is quiet and likes to
draw a lot. She's a good
artist. Everyone thinks so.
I think she has her own
notebook, like I do. Sometimes
I see her writing in it.

Max has braces like Nadia.
He can be nice, but also
very wild. He just moved
here last month so he's new
like me,

Amy and Franny are
twins. I can't tell
them apart, but
Mr. Nudel can.
It must be great
to be a twin.
Then wherever
you go, your best
~~freind~~ friend goes
with you.

I keep making this stupid
mistake. Leah told me a rhyme to help remember whether it's ei or ie. It goes like this: I before E except after C or when sounded like A as in neighbor or weigh.

I brought my notebook with me to school so I can write down things to remember to tell Nadia. Right now it's lunch time. Today's hot lunch is beef stew, tater gems, canned peach slices, and a brownie. Yucch!

canned peaches, 50 years-old army surplus

cardboardy potatoes (gems?!??)

fossilized brownie from the rocazoic era

milk (ok)

dog food or mud puddle — you pick.

Franklin just mooshed his tater gems. Gross me out! They were disgusting before, but now they look like squashed bugs. Mario flung the cling peaches at Philip (one flung cling peach clung to his head)! Mia used the brownie as a doorstop to keep the cafeteria door open. (A few more brownies and they could build the new gym the teachers are always talking about.)
Lucky for me I'm too busy writing to eat.

Introducing: Cafeteria Foods!!

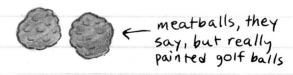

meatballs, they say, but really painted golf balls

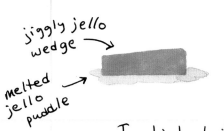
jiggly jello wedge →

melted jello puddle →

round scoop of mashed potato with gluey gooey gravy ←

I did drink the milk, but the beef stew was too disgusting even to smell. Jenna says they use dog food. I believe it!

↑
roll that tastes like a cotton ball

The only kid who ate everything was Melissa. She says food here is lots better than what she gets at home. She even helps the hair-net ladies so she can have seconds.

fishstick, either soggy or crunchy, never just right, if there is a just right for fish sticks.
↑

Definitely DO NOT EAT
↓

Deee-licious!

Yum!

Yum!

And what are those green things? And what it food is the mystery. Why they call it food is the mystery. mystery casserole
↓

From now on, I'm bringing my lunch.

↖ Once upon a time, these were green beans. Now they're soggy rubber bands.

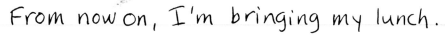

Every Sunday, Mom lets me call Nadia, and we can talk for 10 minutes. Nadia says she misses me, too. I told her about my notebook, how I write down things to tell her and draw pictures. She says I should write stories in my notebook, not just things I notice. I don't know. Nadia makes up great stories. I just like to draw pictures.

I got a letter from Nadia today. It says:

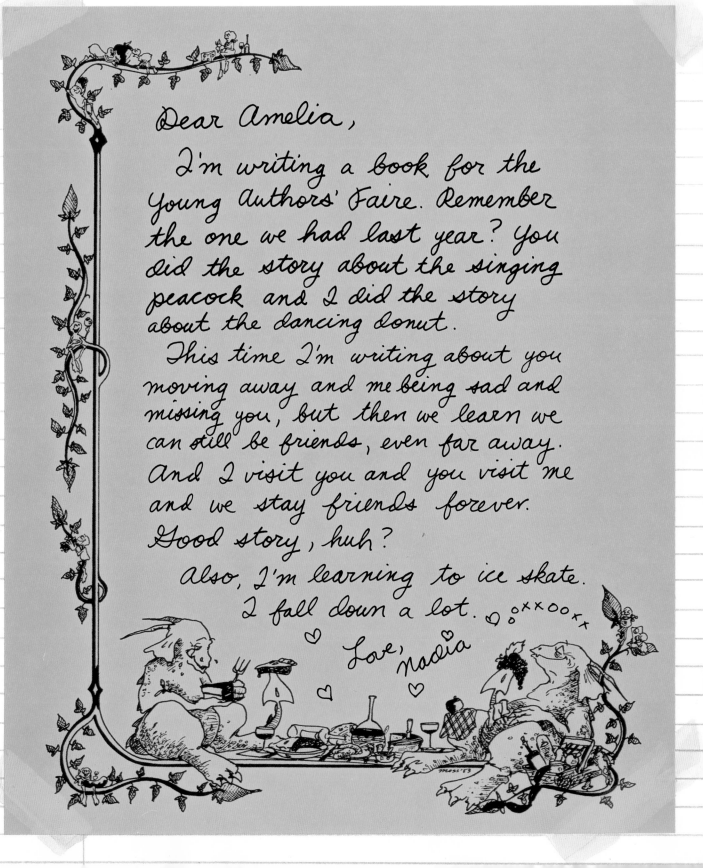

Dear Amelia,

I'm writing a book for the Young Authors' Faire. Remember the one we had last year? You did the story about the singing peacock and I did the story about the dancing donut.

This time I'm writing about you moving away and me being sad and missing you, but then we learn we can still be friends, even far away. And I visit you and you visit me and we stay friends forever. Good story, huh?

Also, I'm learning to ice skate. I fall down a lot. ♡ °xxooxx

Love,
Nadia

This school has an Authors' Faire, too, but I'm not sure I can write a story for it. I can't write about moving away now because Nadia is doing that, and I don't want to be a copycat.

I wish I could learn to ice skate, too, but Mom says no, it's too expensive.

fancy laces

fancy boot →

↑
fancy skate

money flying away

This isn't water. It's ice. →

Maybe I'll write a story about an ice skater instead.

Once there was a girl who wanted to be an Ice Queen. She practiced skating every day. After a long time and lots of practice, she was very good. She could jump and twirl and kick high, all while skating. For her birthday

This kid loses.

This kid wins

she had a skating party. Kids skated for Pin-the-tail-on-the-donkey. They skated for musical chairs. Then they ate cake and ice cream. The girl wore a Birthday Crown. At last her dream had come true. She was the Ice Queen!

Pink sugar roses

Birthday cake, chocolate, of course

Lots of fancy presents

It's an ok story, but not good enough for the Authors' Faire. I'll have to keep trying.

This kid really loses!

← closed door shut in my face

KNOCK FIRST

Cleo has a new best friend already! They close the door to her room and gab, gab, blab, blab for hours. When they go into the kitchen for a snack, they don't even say "Hi" to me. They act like I'm another chair, not a person.

Cleo's friend's name is Gigi. And of course she's very pretty, with pierced ears (which Mom says Cleo and I can't have yet — and definitely no nose piercing ever).

Gigi

Gigi thinks Cleo is so great when really she isn't at all.
   Like watch Cleo eat sometime. You'll see what I mean.

pierced ear with earring

cool tie-dye shirt Gigi got on Telegraph Ave. in Berkeley.

Polite Gigi. She likes carrots.

Polite mouth chewing. Closed, of course.

Gigi eats one tiny nibble at a time. She bites, chews, swallows, and then bites again. It's a very polite way to eat.

But Cleo gobbles. She bites, chews, bites, chews. Finally she has a huge wad in her cheek which she chews, chews, chews, (like a COW!) and when she swallows at last you can see a big bulge go down her throat.

rude mouth chewing (open, of course, so you can see everything), chewing, chewing, chewing, crumbs falling out even. Yuucch!

Cleo

lump of food

crumbs →

Hamburger, her favorite boooooring food.

squashed
bug—
ooops!

Cleo has been sneaking peeks at my notebook, and she's mad at me because of what I wrote about her. <u>Serves her right!</u> She shouldn't read my private business.

So Cleo if you are reading this right now —

BUG OFF

and

STAY OUT

PRIVATE

UNPICKABLE

TOP SECRET

CAUTION:
READING THIS
MATERIAL MAY
BE HAZARDOUS
TO YOUR HEALTH.

SPECIAL FINGERPRINT
PAPER
Your prints are being
recorded NOW!

I'm thinking of another story for the Authors' Faire. Maybe I'll write about Cleo - that would be a comedy!

Nadia says she asked our teacher (really her teacher, my old teacher, Mrs. Kim) if I could have a book in their Faire, too, and she said yes! So now I need to make two books —or one book twice. (Twin books like Amy and Franny.)

I like the idea of having my story next to Nadia's.

↑
stamp
for
a Nadia
letter -
Fish
you
were
here!

Nadia says I write great letters, so I can write a great story. I say it's not the same.

← This is how I drew hands when I was little.

I start to write, but then things get in the way. Like suddenly I notice my hand that's doing the writing, and I start thinking, why are hands so wrinkly? Why do we have a thumb? Why 5 fingers and not 4 or 6? Isn't it amazing how our fingers move and how many things they can do?

This isn't nail polish. It's marker.

Hands are very hard to draw. It takes lots of practice.

Once Nadia colored her fingernails with marker. I stole some of Cleo's Purple Passion Nail Polish and painted my fingernails and toenails.

It looked great except when I was about to eat something, sometimes I forgot I had painted my fingernails, and I'd think I was about to eat a grape with whatever I was eating.

grape

peanut

grape

Toes look like grapes now.

Cleo was mad at me for a whole week, but it was worth it.

It was Nadia's birthday yesterday. We used to celebrate our birthdays together since they're only a week apart, but not this time. Nadia called me on the phone (even though it wasn't Sunday) and told me about her party, and the cake, and all the presents. It made me cry. I wanted to be there so much. Nadia said she's sending me a prize bag and one of the candles from the cake. Of course she can't send a piece of cake itself, it would arrive all in crumbs, so she drew a picture instead so I could see how nice it was.

It looked beautiful.

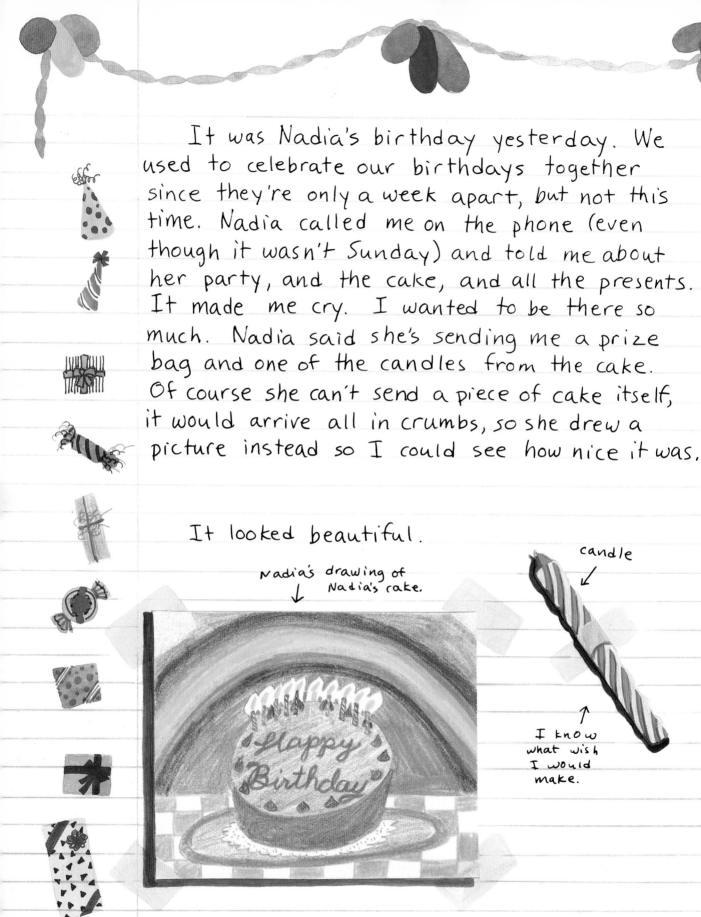

Nadia's drawing of
Nadia's cake.
↓

candle
↓

↑
I know
what wish
I would
make.

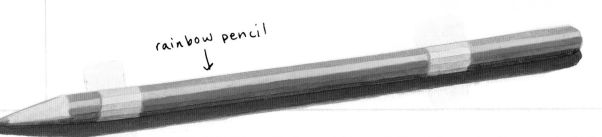
rainbow pencil

This was in the prize bag with the other stuff on this page.

I sent her a present, but she said she hasn't gotten it yet. It's a Do-It-Yourself Experiment Kit. Because Nadia loves doing experiments. So do I. I wish I could do the kit with her, but I can't. Mom says I can visit her during summer vacation, but that's a long way off. By then she'll have done all the experiments.

prize bag

I got Nadia's prize bag today. I'm keeping it here so it will last forever.

← ring

← eraser shaped like ice cream cone.

↑ stickers

party thing you blow on to make TOOOT sound

I was drawing on the chalkboard today during recess because I felt too sad to go out and play. I drew Nadia the way I remember her. Once I drew her face on the blackboard at my old school, and she saw it and hated it. She said I made her nose look like a faucet, but really that's how it looks. Noses just look funny, that's all. Even on princesses.

Nadia—she didn't like how I drew her hair either.

softee icecream hair

tiara crown

dainty delicate princess nose

← yum, yum. slurp!

diamond earrings

pearls

Drawing of Nadia →

If you really look at noses, this is really how they are.

Nose Page

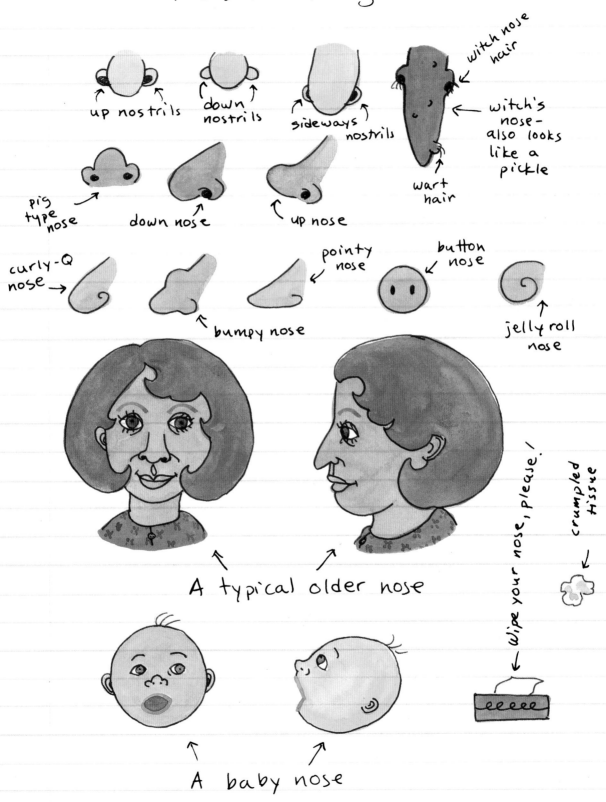

up nostrils

down nostrils

sideways nostrils

with nose hair

witch's nose - also looks like a pickle

wart hair

pig type nose

down nose

up nose

curly-Q nose

bumpy nose

pointy nose

button nose

jelly roll nose

A typical older nose

Wipe your nose, please!

crumpled tissue

A baby nose

A girl from my class, her name is Leah, she saw me drawing all my noses and came to watch me. She said I'm a really good artist. I said she's famous for being a <u>great</u> artist in our school. She said she had a new set of markers and watercolor paints and would I like to go to her house after school and draw with her? Would I !!

Nadia will always be my friend, but now she's a far-away friend. I need a close-by friend, too. Someone I can invite to my birthday party, if I even have a birthday party.

me, on my birthday — if I had a party, who would come?

← party bow in hair

← party dress

There's a bow in back, too.

cinnamon, my old Teddy Bear

my old Raggedy Ann doll

my old Pig Pal

They can come to my party.

— party tights

← party shoes that make a tap tap sound when you walk

colored pencil

crayon

marker

paint brush

Leah has a nice room with a giant bulletin board covered with her drawings and paintings. She's very good, that's for sure. I made good pictures at her house, too. My favorite shows me and Nadia and Leah all having a picnic together under a rainbow.

my favorite drawing

places for mixing new colors

Leah has markers, paints, crayons, and colored pencils. I used them all in this one picture.

paints — great colors!

place for brushes

I finally wrote my story for the Authors' Faire at my old school and my new school. Here it is:

Once there was a girl who wanted a cloud for a pet. It would be soft and fluffy and cuddly and it wouldn't make messes on the rug. But she didn't know how to catch a cloud. She tried using a net. No luck. She tried a fishing pole, cast in the sky. Nope. She just couldn't reach high enough. She tried flying a kite with sticky glue on it. A cloud could stick to the glue, she thought, but no cloud did.

sticky glue

So she decided to pretend that all the clouds were hers, and she kept them in the sky so they could float around. Whenever she wanted one, she whistled and a cloud would cozy up for a pet and a cuddle.

She gave them names like Snowpup, Fifferfluff, Hushball, and Mistmuzz.

And when she had to move far away, to a new house, a new school, a new city, the clouds came with her. They followed wherever she went!

On her birthday, they gave her a big cloud party with rainbow cake, and she was very happy.

The End

↑
a slice of
rainbow cake
with cloud
frosting

rocketship ride

ADMIT ONE ← I've got a ticket to RIIIIDE and I don't care!

BIG BALLOON ↓

saturn ↑

Jupiter with its Red Spot ↑

Mom says for my birthday I can invite one friend and we'll go to Space World together. We can go on all the rides we want and eat cotton candy and buy big balloons.

I asked Leah, and she said Yes! It's not the same as a party with Nadia, but still, it's pretty good.

Nadia called, and she said she got my present and my cloud story, and she loves them both. And she's saving the Experiment Kit to do with me when I visit her!

She says she misses me. "Write to me," she says. "Draw me more pictures." I promise I will and I tell her I miss her, too.

← bubbling test tube from Experiment Kit

mysterious powders to mix in test tube →

I have a GREAT idea! I'll send her a new story, complete with pictures. I just have to write one. But HELP! There's no more room. This is the last page of my notebook. I better tell Mom that's what I want for my birthday. A Brand New Notebook!

Allston Branch Library
00 North Harvard Street
Allston, MA 02135